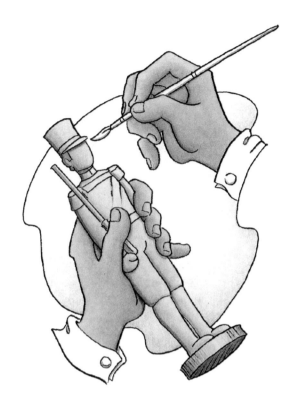

The Brave Toy Soldier

Based upon The Steadfast Tin Soldier,
a fairy tale by Hans Christian Andersen

Published by UMI (Urban Ministries, Inc.)
Chicago, Illinois
Text and illustrations copyright © 2006 by UMI (Urban Ministries, Inc.)

Library of Congress Control Number: 2006907098
Hardcover Library of Congress Control Number: 2006936864
ISBN 10: 1-932715-82-7
Hardcover ISBN 10: 1-934056-20-0
ISBN 13: 978-1-932715-82-8
Hardcover ISBN 13: 978-1-934056-20-2

Produced by Color-Bridge Books, LLC
Printed in the U.S.A.

The Brave Toy Soldier

Retold and Illustrated by
Fred Crump, Jr.

Urban Ministries, Inc.

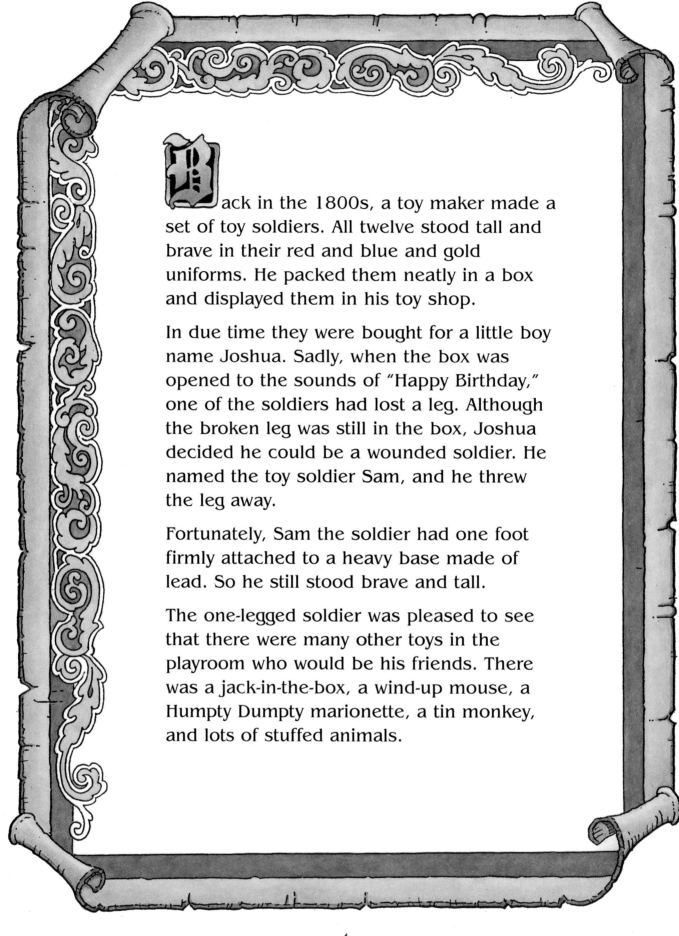

ack in the 1800s, a toy maker made a set of toy soldiers. All twelve stood tall and brave in their red and blue and gold uniforms. He packed them neatly in a box and displayed them in his toy shop.

In due time they were bought for a little boy name Joshua. Sadly, when the box was opened to the sounds of "Happy Birthday," one of the soldiers had lost a leg. Although the broken leg was still in the box, Joshua decided he could be a wounded soldier. He named the toy soldier Sam, and he threw the leg away.

Fortunately, Sam the soldier had one foot firmly attached to a heavy base made of lead. So he still stood brave and tall.

The one-legged soldier was pleased to see that there were many other toys in the playroom who would be his friends. There was a jack-in-the-box, a wind-up mouse, a Humpty Dumpty marionette, a tin monkey, and lots of stuffed animals.

Sam, The Wounded Soldier

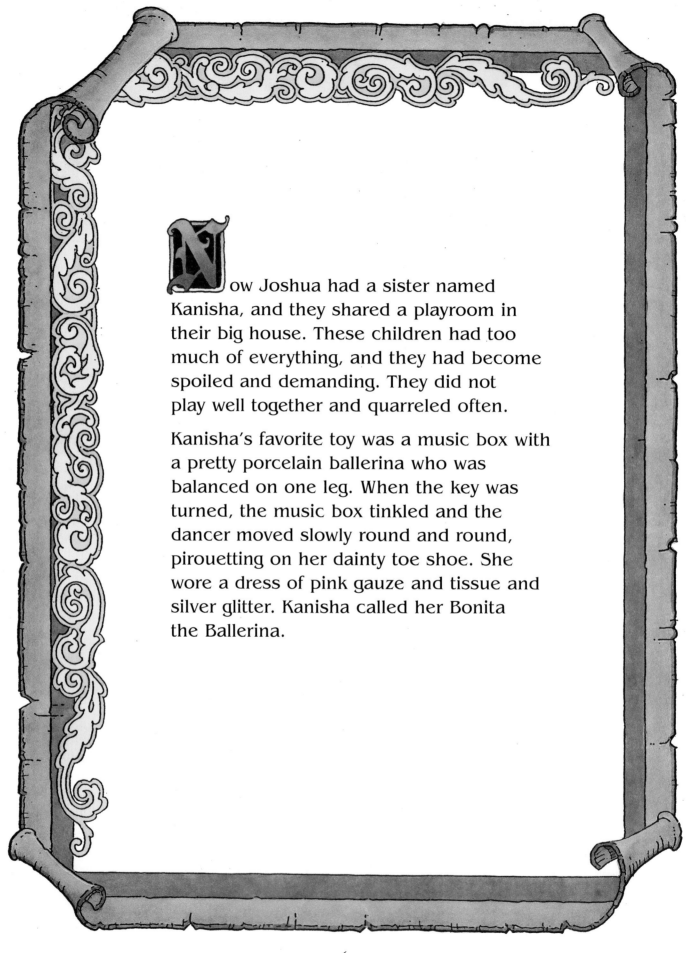

ow Joshua had a sister named Kanisha, and they shared a playroom in their big house. These children had too much of everything, and they had become spoiled and demanding. They did not play well together and quarreled often.

Kanisha's favorite toy was a music box with a pretty porcelain ballerina who was balanced on one leg. When the key was turned, the music box tinkled and the dancer moved slowly round and round, pirouetting on her dainty toe shoe. She wore a dress of pink gauze and tissue and silver glitter. Kanisha called her Bonita the Ballerina.

Love At First Sight

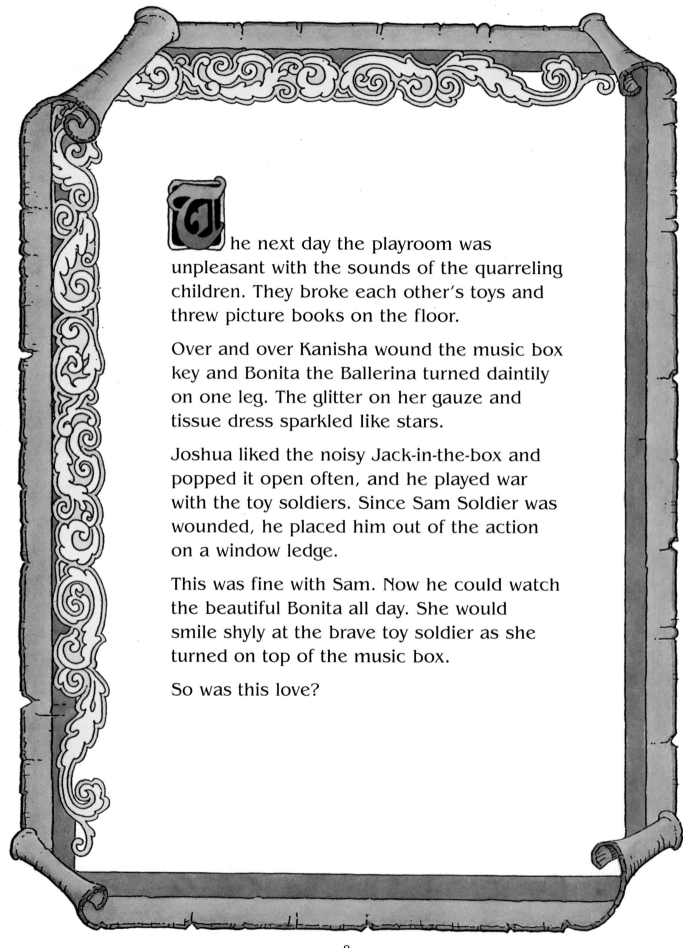

The next day the playroom was unpleasant with the sounds of the quarreling children. They broke each other's toys and threw picture books on the floor.

Over and over Kanisha wound the music box key and Bonita the Ballerina turned daintily on one leg. The glitter on her gauze and tissue dress sparkled like stars.

Joshua liked the noisy Jack-in-the-box and popped it open often, and he played war with the toy soldiers. Since Sam Soldier was wounded, he placed him out of the action on a window ledge.

This was fine with Sam. Now he could watch the beautiful Bonita all day. She would smile shyly at the brave toy soldier as she turned on top of the music box.

So was this love?

Bonita Ballerina smiled

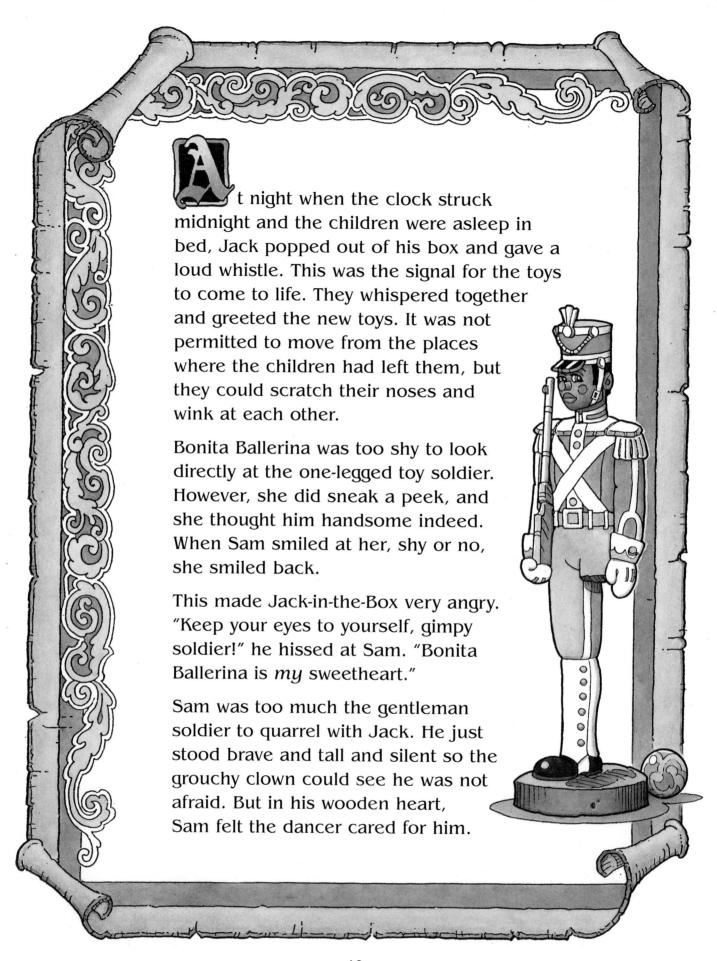

At night when the clock struck midnight and the children were asleep in bed, Jack popped out of his box and gave a loud whistle. This was the signal for the toys to come to life. They whispered together and greeted the new toys. It was not permitted to move from the places where the children had left them, but they could scratch their noses and wink at each other.

Bonita Ballerina was too shy to look directly at the one-legged toy soldier. However, she did sneak a peek, and she thought him handsome indeed. When Sam smiled at her, shy or no, she smiled back.

This made Jack-in-the-Box very angry. "Keep your eyes to yourself, gimpy soldier!" he hissed at Sam. "Bonita Ballerina is *my* sweetheart."

Sam was too much the gentleman soldier to quarrel with Jack. He just stood brave and tall and silent so the grouchy clown could see he was not afraid. But in his wooden heart, Sam felt the dancer cared for him.

Jack-in-the-Box was Grouchy

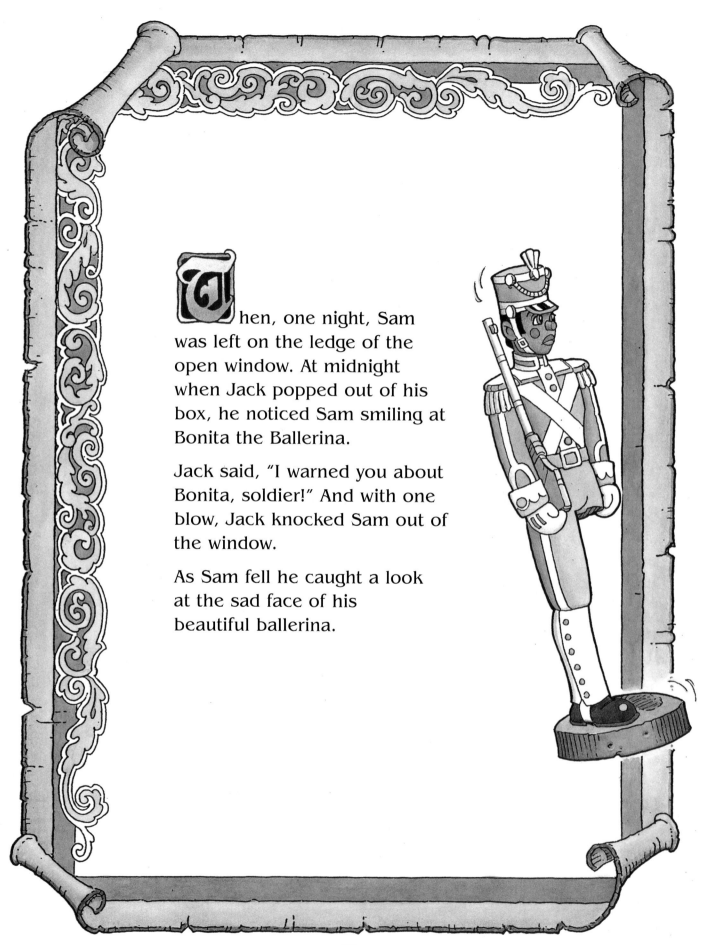

Then, one night, Sam was left on the ledge of the open window. At midnight when Jack popped out of his box, he noticed Sam smiling at Bonita the Ballerina.

Jack said, "I warned you about Bonita, soldier!" And with one blow, Jack knocked Sam out of the window.

As Sam fell he caught a look at the sad face of his beautiful ballerina.

He hit Sam Soldier

hankfully, Sam landed in the grass and did not break his one good leg. But Sam could not move, and soon it began to rain.

A big ugly frog grumped at him and made his wooden heart thump. Sam knew a soldier must be brave, so he stayed silent and did not cry out. And the frog left him lying in the pouring rain.

A Frog grumped at him

he next day, a boy who was passing by found Sam lying in the grass.

The boy wore a folded paper hat on his head. He took it off and put the toy soldier in it. He used it for a boat to give Sam a ride in the rain water running along the gutter.

Suddenly the paper boat was swept into a sewer drain.

Sam was not at all happy about the darkness and the rushing water.

Sam was in Big Trouble

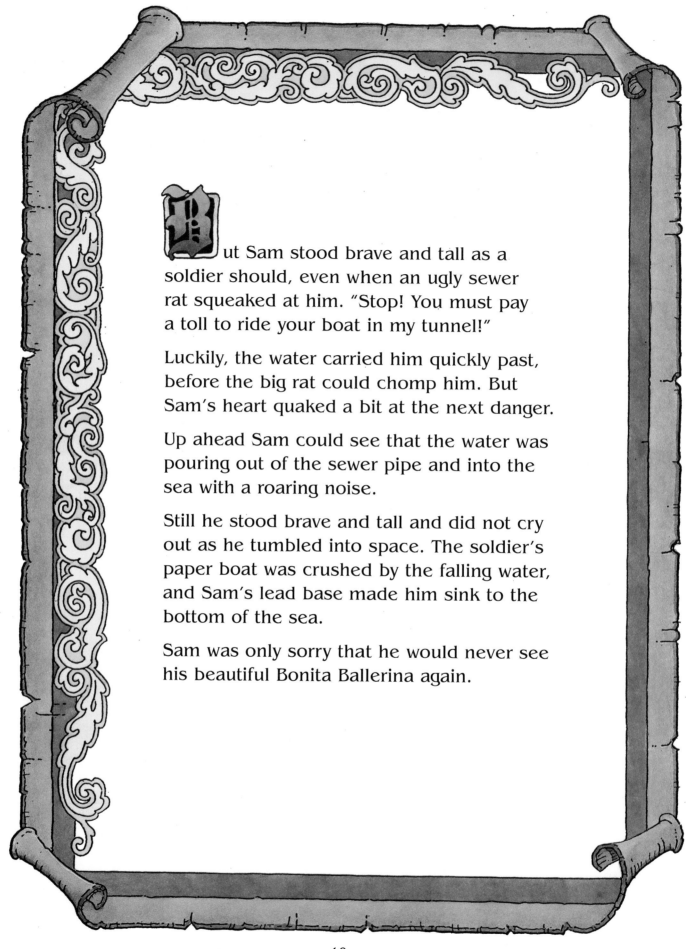

But Sam stood brave and tall as a soldier should, even when an ugly sewer rat squeaked at him. "Stop! You must pay a toll to ride your boat in my tunnel!"

Luckily, the water carried him quickly past, before the big rat could chomp him. But Sam's heart quaked a bit at the next danger.

Up ahead Sam could see that the water was pouring out of the sewer pipe and into the sea with a roaring noise.

Still he stood brave and tall and did not cry out as he tumbled into space. The soldier's paper boat was crushed by the falling water, and Sam's lead base made him sink to the bottom of the sea.

Sam was only sorry that he would never see his beautiful Bonita Ballerina again.

a Grouchy Rat and a Waterfall

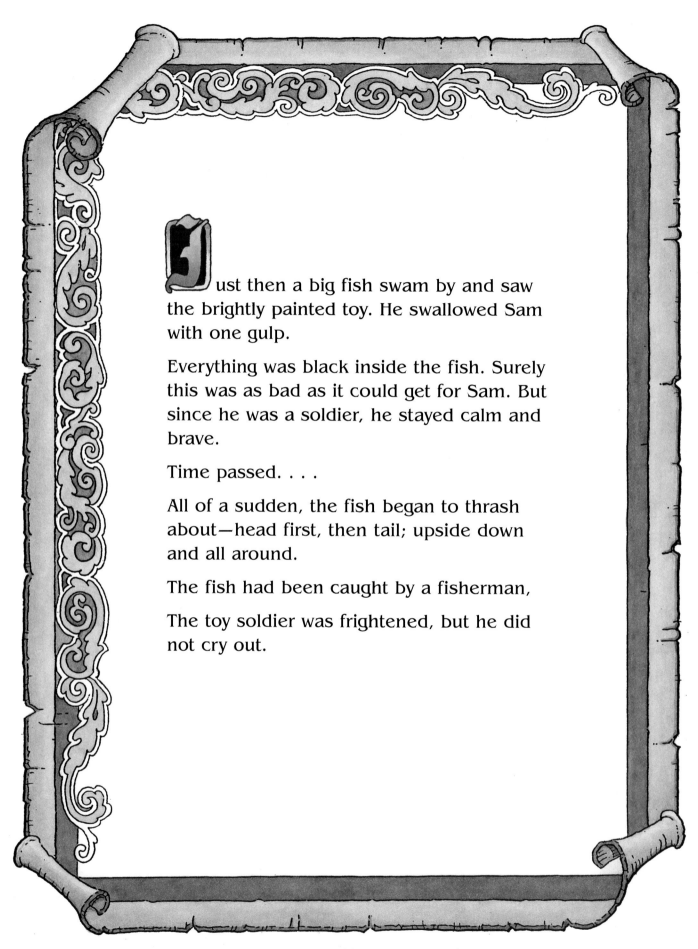

ust then a big fish swam by and saw the brightly painted toy. He swallowed Sam with one gulp.

Everything was black inside the fish. Surely this was as bad as it could get for Sam. But since he was a soldier, he stayed calm and brave.

Time passed. . . .

All of a sudden, the fish began to thrash about—head first, then tail; upside down and all around.

The fish had been caught by a fisherman.

The toy soldier was frightened, but he did not cry out.

Swallowed by a Big Fish

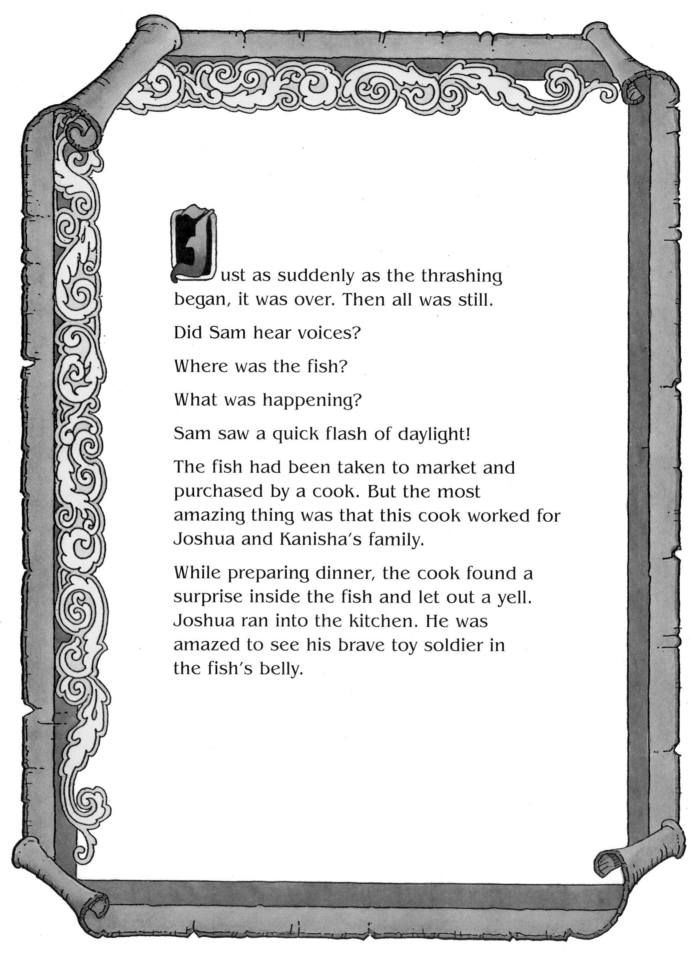

Just as suddenly as the thrashing began, it was over. Then all was still.

Did Sam hear voices?

Where was the fish?

What was happening?

Sam saw a quick flash of daylight!

The fish had been taken to market and purchased by a cook. But the most amazing thing was that this cook worked for Joshua and Kanisha's family.

While preparing dinner, the cook found a surprise inside the fish and let out a yell. Joshua ran into the kitchen. He was amazed to see his brave toy soldier in the fish's belly.

Sam was Home Again

oshua ran to the playroom, carrying his lost, bedraggled toy soldier. "Look Kanisha! What an adventure Sam must have had!"

There were all the toys. There was Bonita. She was very happy to see Sam again.

Sam's wooden heart was pounding with joy. Even Jack looked a bit relieved. After all, he had started the trouble in the first place.

Everyone was happy except Kanisha

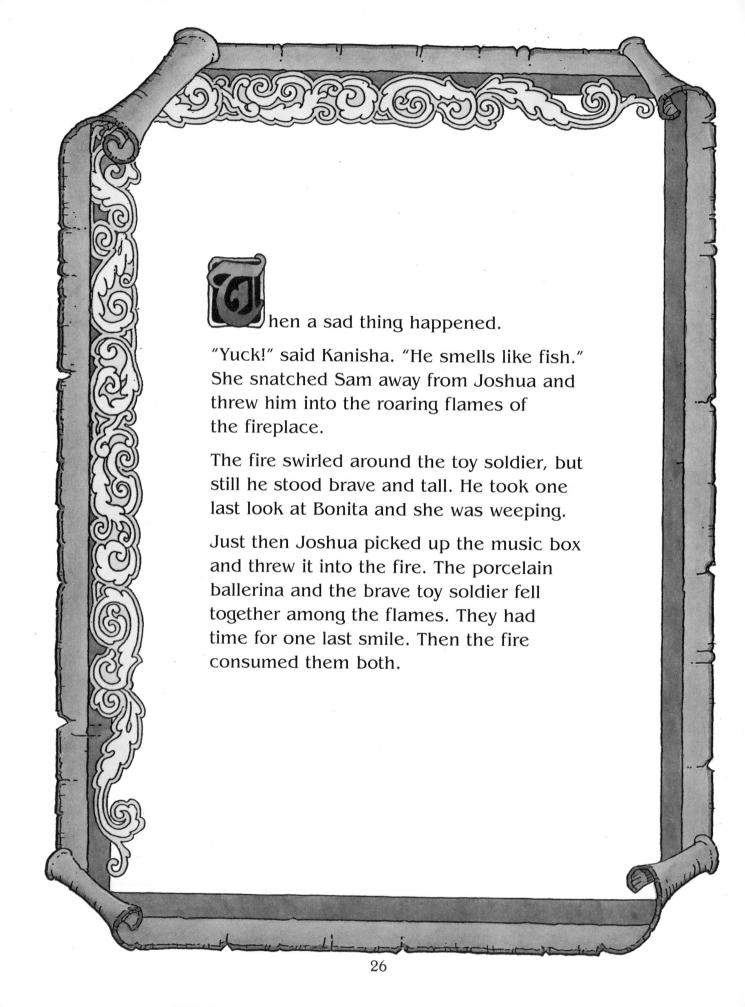

Then a sad thing happened.

"Yuck!" said Kanisha. "He smells like fish." She snatched Sam away from Joshua and threw him into the roaring flames of the fireplace.

The fire swirled around the toy soldier, but still he stood brave and tall. He took one last look at Bonita and she was weeping.

Just then Joshua picked up the music box and threw it into the fire. The porcelain ballerina and the brave toy soldier fell together among the flames. They had time for one last smile. Then the fire consumed them both.

Together at Last

The next day it was very quiet in the playroom. The two children were sad and tearful about their bad behavior with the toys.

Joshua poked around in the cold ashes with a coal scoop. Then he cried out, "Kanisha! Come look!"

He pulled from the ashes a lump of something. The wood and lead and gauze and porcelain and tinsel from the soldier and ballerina had melted into a perfectly shaped heart.

What Have We Done?

The children put the melted heart in a little box lined with red velvet and stood it on the mantel.

And for some reason, this beautiful symbol of love brought calm to the playroom at last.

The children never quarreled or broke their toys again.

A Symbol of Love

rom that time on, whenever a new toy was brought into the playroom, this story was told. Grumpy old Jack-in-the-Box would tell of the love between Sam and Bonita the Ballerina.

And he always ended the tale by saying, "He was truly a brave toy soldier."